W9-BNT-020

Kate Aver Avraham

What Will You Be, Sara Mee?

Illustrated by
Anne Sibley O'Brien

⌂ Charlesbridge

"**What will you be, Sara Mee?**" I ask my baby sister as soon as she wakes up on her first birthday.

"Cho." She reaches out to me and says as much of my name as she can.

She bounces up and down in her crib while I tell her all about the big party we're going to have for her today.

"It's called a *tol,* Mee Mee," I say. "Everyone is coming, just like they did for mine. There will be lots of food and presents. And best of all, a special game, the *toljabee,* to find out what you'll be when you grow up."

Our father, Aboji, hears us and comes in the room.
He picks up my sister and swings her high over
his head.

"Here's my birthday girl!" he says, and kisses her
round-as-the-moon face.

After breakfast I help Omoni, our mother, give my sister a bath. She splashes and splashes and gets me all wet. I give her my toy tugboat to play with. She pushes it in and out of the bubbles.

"*Pppppppppppttttttttt.* . . ." She blows air through her lips to make boat sounds. Omoni and I laugh.

"What will you be, Sara Mee?" I ask her again. "Maybe you'll be the captain of a ship."

"She could be," my mother says. "Girls can be anything in America."

Our grandparents just arrived from Korea a few days ago, so they're still a little tired. When they finally wake up, they hug me and my sister and wish her a happy birthday. "*Saengirul chookahae!*"

They came for my *tol* five years ago, too. That's when they found out what *I* might be when I grow up.

Halmoni, my grandmother, holds my sister on her lap and dresses her in the silk *hanbok* she sewed just for today's party.

"Eeeeeee!" Sara Mee squeals with delight when she sees the rainbow stripes on the sleeves. She waves her arms up and down like a bird.

I tickle her under her flapping wings and ask again, "What will you be, Sara Mee?"

"You love the bright cloth so much, granddaughter," Halmoni says. "Maybe you will make beautiful clothes someday."

Soon, people begin to arrive for the party. I get to answer the door.

Auntie Jung and Auntie Lee are first, carrying plates full of the food they've been cooking—some of my very favorites like *pulgogi*, spicy *kimchi*, and rice cakes.

"How pretty you look, niece." My aunties pick up Sara Mee and kiss her silky, black hair.

When they set her down, she toddles over to the table, reaches up, grabs a whole rice cake, and starts to stuff it in her mouth.

"What a little piggy, Mee Mee," I tell her. Then I feed her the rice cake one bite at a time.

Auntie Lee chuckles. "What will you be, Sara Mee? You know good food when you see it! Maybe you'll be a cook like your aunties."

"Or a chef in a fancy restaurant," Auntie Jung says.

Next, Uncle Kwang arrives with his *janggo* drum.

"Big day, huh?" he says in his booming voice as he ruffles my hair. Then he begins to play, and Omoni strums along on her *kayagum*.

When my sister hears the music, she claps her hands and sings made-up words. Uncle Kwang laughs. He sets the drum down and puts my sister on his knee.

"And what will you be, Miss Sara Mee?" he asks loudly. "I think you'll be a musician like Uncle."

I answer the door many times. Friends and neighbors and cousins arrive. Everyone is eating and talking, talking and eating. I get tired of waiting and go to my mother.

"Omma! When are we going to play the prophecy game?"

"Very soon, Chong," she reassures me.

Finally everyone is there. My grandfather, Haraboji, carries Sara Mee to a special low table in the living room. When he tries to set her down, she clings to him and howls.

Halmoni rubs my sister's back and tells her, "You have the strong spirit of Tiger in the Green Mountains. Maybe you'll be a great leader someday. But you must learn when to growl and when to purr."

"I didn't cry like that at my *tol,* Mee Mee," I tell my sister.

Halmoni laughs. "No, grandson. You cried even louder!"

My sister stops crying. Haraboji sets her on a pile of
soft cushions on the floor behind the low table.

My parents sit on either side of Sara Mee, and I get to sit across the table in the very front. Everyone else gathers around us to watch.

Haraboji brings out a polished cherrywood box that has been in our family for many generations. Halmoni turns the latch and lifts the lid. Then, they both look at me and nod.

I can't believe it! I get to help. I look at my baby sister.
"Here we go, Mee Mee," I say.

I reach into the box. The first thing my hand touches is a toy bow-and-arrow set. I lift it out carefully and set it on the table.

"Will you be a soldier?" Haraboji asks my sister.

I reach in again and lay a paintbrush on the table.
"Will you be an artist?" Halmoni asks.

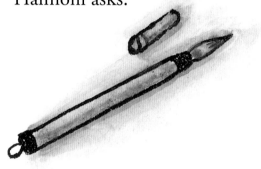

Next, I pull out a little bag of gold coins and pour them onto the table.

"Will you be successful in business?" Haraboji asks.

I continue to lift out objects: a book, a spoon, and some yarn. Haraboji and Halmoni take turns asking my sister if she'll be a scholar, a cook, or will she live a long time.

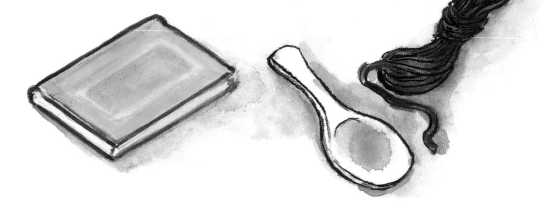

When I reach in and pull out a bottle of ink, I blurt out, "I know this one!"

Haraboji smiles and says, "Go ahead, grandson."

"Will you be a writer?" I ask proudly.

After everything is out of the box on the table in front of
my sister, I say one more time, "What will you be, Sara Mee?"

Everyone leans in closer. We are very quiet as we wait and watch.

We don't have to wait long. My sister's little hand shoots out across the table. She grabs the paintbrush and waves it around in the air.

"Ahhhhhh!" we all exclaim at the same time.

When the game is over and the presents are unwrapped, everyone goes back to eating and talking, talking and eating. Everyone except my baby sister and me. I put a big pad of paper and fat crayons down on the table. Sara Mee grabs a red crayon and starts scribbling.

"That's it, Mee Mee," I tell her.
I pick up a marker and write words to
go with what she's drawing.

Glossary

aboji: father

Chong Chol: a famous classic Korean poet, 1536–1593

halmoni: grandmother

hanbok: Literally means Korean costume, and includes all traditional Korean dress.
Tolbok is the traditional dress for the first birthday. A girl's *tolbok* is usually
made of brightly colored silk and consists of a striped jacket and
long, red skirt.

haraboji: grandfather

janggo: A two-headed drum shaped like an hourglass, with hide
stretched over the heads. It is struck with a bamboo stick,
a wooden mallet, or the hand. One of the most popular musical
instruments in Korea, it is often played to accompany dancing.

kayagum: A long, twelve-stringed instrument, held
on the lap and plucked with the fingers.
It was designed to sound similar to
the human voice.

kimchi: A traditional and very popular spicy,
pickled vegetable dish made with cabbage and
radish or cucumber. In ancient Korea, *kimchi* was kept in large earthenware jars
and buried underground to keep it cold and fresh all winter.

mee: beautiful

omma: mom

omoni: mother

pulgogi: One of the most popular meat dishes in Korea. It is made of marinated strips
of beef that are charcoal roasted (barbecued), often right at the dinner table.

saengirul chookahae: happy birthday

tol: The traditional first-birthday celebration for a Korean child. It includes many guests, a feast, gifts for the child, and the ritual event of the *toljabee*. In ancient Korea, this was an especially joyous occasion because, sadly, many babies did not survive even one year. Today the tradition of the *tol* continues in Korea, in America for Korean Americans, and also in other Asian countries, such as China.

toljabee: The prophecy game played at a child's *tol* (first birthday), in which symbolic items are placed on a table in front of the child. What the child picks first (and sometimes second) are supposed to predict his or her future.

Author's Note

My daughter, Sara Mee Jung Kim, arrived at the San Francisco airport aboard a Korean Air jumbo jet on September 14, 1984, thus beginning the multicultural journey of love that has so enriched my life. One of the many Korean customs my family shared with Sara Mee was the *tol,* or first-birthday celebration. An ancient custom that was performed to predict a child's future, the *tol* is still celebrated in Korea, and many Korean Americans and adoptive families like mine recognize it. I hope this book will not only bring the *tol* into the lives of readers but will also encourage people to learn about and share in the first-birthday prophecy customs that exist in many other cultures around the world.

My special thanks to Dr. Byung-Joon Lim, Professor and Chairman of the Korean language department at the Defense Language Institute in Monterey, California, for reading the manuscript and making corrections to the Korean. My heartfelt gratitude to Paul, Carol, and Judy, for their guidance and belief in the book.

For my own Sara Mee and in memory of
her brother, Nathan—K. A. A.

For the Park family, three generations—A. S. O'B.

Text copyright © 2010 by Kate Aver Avraham
Illustrations copyright © 2010 by Anne Sibley O'Brien

Published by Charlesbridge
85 Main Street
Watertown, MA 02472
(617) 926-0329
www.charlesbridge.com

Library of Congress Cataloging-in-Publication Data
Avraham, Kate Aver.
   What will you be, Sara Mee? / Kate Aver Avraham ; illustrated by Anne
Sibley O'Brien.
      p. cm.
   Summary: At her *tol,* the first-birthday party, Sara Mee plays the traditional Korean prophecy game—
toljabee—while her extended family and friends watch.
   ISBN 978-1-58089-210-0 (reinforced for library use)
   ISBN 978-1-58089-211-7 (softcover)
[1. Birthdays—Fiction. 2. Parties—Fiction. 3. Brothers and sisters—Fiction.
4. Korean Americans—Fiction.] I. O'Brien, Anne Sibley, ill. II. Title.
PZ7.A955Wh 2010
[E]—dc22   2009001708

Printed in China
(hc) 10 9 8 7 6 5 4 3 2 1
(sc) 10 9 8 7 6 5 4 3 2 1

Illustrations done in ink brushline with watercolor on Arches paper
Display type and text type set in Leaf Filled and Adobe Garamond Pro
Color separations by Chroma Graphics, Singapore
Manufactured by Regent Publishing Services, Hong Kong
Printed September 2009 in ShenZhen, Guangdong, China
Production supervision by Brian G. Walker
Designed by Susan Mallory Sherman